Ticket to Tallinn

John Hare

Series Editor: John McRae

Nelson

Thomas Nelson and Sons Ltd
Nelson House Mayfield Road
Walton-on-Thames Surrey
KT12 5PL UK

51 York Place
Edinburgh
EH1 3JD UK

Thomas Nelson (Hong Kong) Ltd
Toppan Building 10/F
22A Westlands Road
Quarry Bay Hong Kong

© John Hare 1993

First published by Thomas Nelson and Sons Ltd 1993

ISBN 0-17-5562938
NPN 9 8 7 6 5 4 3 2 1

Illustrations by Trevor Smith

All rights reserved. No part of this publication may be reproduced, copied or transmitted save with written permission or in accordance with the provisions of the Copyright, Design and Patents Act 1988, or under the terms of any licence permitting limited copying issued by the Copyright Licensing Agency, 90 Tottenham Court Road, London W1P 9HE.
Any person who does any unauthorised act in relation to this publication may be liable to criminal prosecution and civil claims for damages.

Printed in Hong Kong

Chapter 1
This is Roger

'Is it a deal?'

Peter extended his hand across the table and accidentally knocked over a coffee cup. Coffee spilt on to the papers in front of him.

'It's a deal,' murmured Peter, grasping the other man's fleshy hand as the coffee dripped down his thigh.

Galina started dabbing at the stains on his trousers with a yellow duster. 'So sorry, Mister Peter. So sorry.' But Peter was oblivious of the coffee, his trousers or Galina. He looked up at the unattractive face of the man opposite him with its bushy eyebrows, puffy eyes and thirty-six hour stubble. 'I am sure our venture will be a great success,' he said.

Victor Bogdanov gave Peter a crooked grin and reached for an unopened bottle of vodka on the cupboard beside him. 'Let us drink to this success,' he said.

As he opened the bottle, Galina laughed nervously and took two empty glasses out of a cupboard.

'Nothing for you, Galina?' growled Victor, holding the bottle over her head. 'Nothing for you by way of celebration?'

Galina smiled coyly and reached for a third glass. She was an attractive, plump, middle-aged lady, who obviously took great pride in her appearance, despite the

3

Ticket to Tallinn

This is Roger

drabness of her surroundings. Her face was carefully made up, and her skirt and expensive jumper had quite clearly not been purchased in the USSR. And neither had the three chunky gold rings which she wore on three separate fingers on her left hand.

Victor winked at her and again extended his hand towards Peter. He was overweight and overindulgent in the vodka and delicacies that he was able to obtain quite easily in the thriving black market for successful bureaucrats. His head was bald, and in striking contrast to the hand which he now held out for Peter to grasp; this was covered in thick, curly, black hair which extended well beyond his knuckles and up to the joint of each finger. Peter gripped the hairy hand firmly.

That evening, in the sparsely furnished bedroom of his Moscow hotel, he studied the document which he had signed which designated him the sole European distributor of Khakhlamo woodware; these were beautifully carved and painted items ranging from tiny boxes to heavily decorated tables and chairs. He put the agreement to one side, picked up the thick, heavily illustrated catalogue and turning the pages slowly he carefully studied each item in turn. His last doubts vanished. I am going to be rich, he thought.

Next morning Victor arrived punctually at eight o'clock to take him to the run-down offices of the COP, the Centre for Overseas Projects. His smart, chauffeur driven, dark blue Volvo estate car stood out in stark contrast to the ageing Russian vehicles, which belched thick black exhaust fumes all around them. Peter wondered how the COP had managed to purchase such a car. Some foreign exchange fiddle, he thought.

As they drove off, Peter could see long queues forming outside food shops on either side of the street – most basic essentials were in short supply. 'They queue for hours,' said Victor, sensing his unspoken thoughts. 'When they reach the top of the queue, they often have to go to the back and start all over again.'

'Why is that?'

'They are only allowed to queue for one item at a time,' replied Victor, leaning towards him. Not for the first time, Peter recoiled from the smell of Victor's breath and rotting teeth. It was unfortunate that the breath of his principal host, interpreter and potential business colleague should be in such a state. It made normal conversation quite an ordeal!

The driver suddenly swerved to avoid a large pot-hole in the road. As he did so he inadvertently drove through a large puddle and splashed an old woman with dirty, muddy water. She shook her fist at them and shouted something unintelligible in Russian.

Victor laughed. 'The transition to a market economy affects us all in different ways,' he said. 'Even that woman is experiencing the side-effects by being splashed by a foreign car.'

Peter, who thought that the joke was neither funny nor witty, said nothing but felt, not for the first time, a slight twinge of uneasiness at the sense of values of his business partner.

Before long they were outside the rusting gates of the entrance to the COP and the driver was sounding his horn impatiently for someone to come and open them.

Eventually, an old man shuffled out of a wooden hut and slowly unlocked the large padlock. He looked down at his feet as they passed through the open gates, showing no sign of friendliness or recognition. A few minutes later they were walking up the four flights of stairs to the COP offices.

'I must apologise once again that the lift is still out of order,' said Victor. 'This transitional phase of adjustment to free market forces is difficult for us all.' By the time they had reached the third landing he was puffing and panting and in need of a rest. 'You go on ahead,' he said to Peter, 'just let me pause here to get my breath back.'

Peter climbed up the remaining flight of stairs and knocked at a door which had 'Centre for Overseas Projects' written both in Russian and English. The door was flung open and he was overwhelmed by Galina.

'Good morning, Mister Peter. How are you? How did you sleep? My English is good, no?'

'Your English is good – yes,' replied Peter with a laugh, as he kissed her warmly on both cheeks. 'Your English is very good, Galina.' Luckily, Galina had no problem with her breath, and Peter, who had taken a great liking to her, kissed her enthusiastically again.

'I have a surprise for you today,' whispered Galina excitedly. 'I have a companion for your entertainment tonight.'

'Who?'

'My daughter.'

'But you are so young. She must be much too young for me!'

Ticket to Tallinn

Galina put her finger to her mouth, and moments later Victor came through the door, puffing and panting and muttering. 'Those stairs get steeper every day, Galina. You must do something about them.'

'You are getting older and drinking too much vodka every day,' said Galina cheekily. 'If you asked for the lift to be repaired, then you wouldn't have a problem.'

The hours passed quickly as Victor, Peter and Galina discussed the project which had brought Peter to the Centre in Moscow. Peter worked with the International Committee for Environmental Protection. The main purpose of his visit to the USSR was to try to finalise the arrangements for a visit of international experts who would assess the environmental damage which had occurred as a result of the Chernobyl disaster. Most of the current statistical information on that terrible catastrophe was connected with the radiation effects on human beings. The impact on the environment was unknown; the long-term effects barely understood.

After visiting Chernobyl it was planned that the team of experts would fly on to Tallinn in Estonia. There had been persistent rumours that a Soviet nuclear power station, some eighty kilometres from the Baltic state's capital, had had to be shut down to prevent a similar Chernobyl-type catastrophe from taking place. Under the new policy of openness in the Soviet Union, the international team had been given authority to investigate the situation themselves.

Late that afternoon Peter asked the crucial question. 'But when will they be able to make these two visits? The most important point now is for us to agree on a date. We have agreed that the visits to Chernobyl and Tallinn should take place. We have discussed in great detail what will be investigated – but when are the experts going to be allowed to come?'

'I have told you before that it takes time to get the authorisation for such a visit. It is not just one authority that has to give us clearance – there are many.'

'I know that: you have already written to us and explained the problems. But the reason I am here now is because you indicated that a date could be agreed on while I was in Moscow. So when is it to be, this year, next year …?'

'As far as the visit to Chernobyl is concerned, I cannot say. Maybe when you arrive in Tallinn the officials in the environmental department will give you a firm date for that part of the trip. But as for Chernobyl, I am still waiting for clearance from above.'

Peter suddenly became annoyed. 'But this is ridiculous. The team can't make two separate visits, one to Chernobyl and the other to Tallinn. The two visits must be coordinated. You have invited me here to finalise this very point, yet after endless discussion we appear to be no further advanced at all.'

Victor smiled. 'But we are, Mister Peter, we are much further advanced. Haven't we signed an agreement?'

'That agreement is purely personal. It has nothing to do with the main purpose of my visit. It is a joint venture between you and me, and you know that as well as I do.'

'Exactly, so much has been achieved.'

'Are you trying to tell me that the real reason for inviting me to Moscow had nothing to do with either

Chernobyl or Tallinn? Have you really invited me here just to conclude a business partnership between ourselves?'

Victor looked down at his hairy hands. 'I did not say that,' he said quietly.

'No, but you implied it,' continued Peter, realising with rising anger that he was going to have to go back to London without having finalised the most important point of all. He suddenly realised that he was being made to look naïve and foolish.

'Mister Peter,' said Galina softly, 'our country is in turmoil. Nothing is simple. It never has been easy to obtain a bureaucratic decision on anything. Now it is ten times worse. One organisation will approve the visit, another will defer it, another will postpone it. We continually chase our tails – and get nowhere.'

'But we have got somewhere, Mister Peter,' said Victor, looking up and staring at him. 'We are both going to become rich while the bureaucrats dither.'

'Meanwhile, the environment suffers,' responded Peter, caught between self-interest and duty. 'If I had known that you only invited me here to sell your pretty woodware to –'

'The environment will always suffer,' interrupted Victor, 'as long as there are human beings on this earth. I cannot force my people to move faster than they intend to move. The policy changes from one day to the next as various factions gain an upper hand within the system. Even if I had obtained a firm decision for a visit from the experts, it could have been changed before you stepped off the plane.' He looked up and fixed Peter

This is Roger

with a penetrating stare. 'And that is what you will tell your colleagues when you return. You will say that unfortunately, due to the extremely fluid political situation in the USSR, a firm decision was reversed after your arrival. It is as simple as that.'

'Come,' said Galina, 'my daughter has been waiting a long time to meet you. Let's go and see her.'

She looked up at Victor, who gave her, unseen by Peter, a slight nod of his head. Taking hold of Peter's arm, she led him without protest from the room. They walked down the corridor, which was painted, like the rest of the offices, in muddy brown and lemon yellow: colours that seemed to Peter to be entirely appropriate to the general state of the organisation. When they reached a door numbered 'nineteen', Galina knocked and entered without waiting for a reply. Seated with her back to them was a girl bent over a typewriter and dressed in a bright blue dress. She turned towards them, brushing aside her long flowing blonde hair, and rose to her feet.

'Let me introduce my daughter, Natasha,' said Galina, looking expectantly from Peter to Natasha. The girl moved towards him, smiling.

'Hello,' she said, 'I am Natasha Kazakova.'

'Hello,' echoed Peter, 'I am Mister Peter.'

Galina looked anxiously from one to the other. 'Natasha is willing to accompany you to the Moscow State Circus tonight. We have bought tickets for you. Would you like to go?'

'It's a very long time since I've been to a circus,' replied Peter. 'But of course I would love to go. It's the most famous circus in the world.'

This is Roger

'That's good,' said Galina, darting a glance at her daughter. 'Natasha will go back with you to your hotel and then fix a time to pick you up.'

'Come, Mister Peter,' said Natasha brightly. 'I am sure that you have done enough negotiating for today.'

Peter followed her meekly out of the office and down the stairs. He felt not only that he had failed, but also that he had behaved like a fool.

'You are looking sad,' said Natasha as they drove off towards the hotel. 'Is something the matter?'

'No, no. I was just thinking.'

'We could all be very sad here in Russia,' said Natasha quietly. 'There is plenty to be sad about. But we try to keep smiling, so please don't be sad.' Peter looked at her and smiled. 'I am sorry. I will try to be cheerful and forget my problems. Tell me about yourself and why they have asked you to take me to the circus. Is there some secret that you have been told to extract from me by fair means or foul?'

'Fair means or foul? I don't understand.'

'Well, to put it another way, have you, a very attractive girl, been put my way to make me feel comfortable so that you can learn something from me – either by fair methods or,' he paused and winked at her, 'unfair female methods.'

'Aha, now I understand you. The answer is yes/no.'

'What do you mean "yes/no"?'

'Well, "yes", I have been asked to get something from you, but "no," not by what you call "foul means".'

'So you are not a honey trap?'

'A what?'

Ticket to Tallinn

'A honey trap: a pretty girl who has been set up to throw her arms around a helpless, lonely foreigner in order to weaken him to a point where he reveals all.'

'You have been reading too many spy novels,' said Natasha, bursting into laughter.

'I may look innocent,' said Peter, 'but I'm not that innocent. So what is it that you have been asked to extract from me?'

'But that is the game,' said Natasha. 'I try to get it, you try to stop me getting it.'

'But I don't know what it is!'

'That's the fun part.'

'I'm not an important politician or business man, you know. I have no secrets.'

'No, that's true. But you do have something.'

'What?'

Natasha turned away and looked up at the grey sky. 'It's going to snow,' she said. 'It should not be snowing now.'

'That's what we environmentalists mean by "climate change",' said Peter.

'But you needn't worry about the honey trap,' said Natasha. 'That's not a method I am allowed to use because of Vladimir.'

'Vladimir?'

'My boyfriend.'

'Oh, I see.'

'He is coming to the circus with us tonight. You'll meet him then.'

'At the circus?'

'That's right. Do you mind?'

This is Roger

'Of course not. I never intended to fall into your pot of honey, anyway!'

They both laughed.

'I like you,' said Natasha.

'That's good, because I like you too. But where did you learn your English? It's very good.'

'Thank you. I was a tourist guide for a year, working for Intourist. Then one day last month they suddenly said that my English was not good enough, and that they were going to halve my pay.'

'Not good enough! It's nearly perfect.'

Natasha looked Peter in the eyes. 'It was really nothing to do with my English at all. You see, it was my boss's way of making money. He only said it so that he could pocket half my salary. Not one person had complained about my English.'

'But that's terrible. Why didn't you complain?'

'Complain to whom? He was my boss, there was no one else to complain to. And even if there had been they would only have laughed at me and said that I was lucky to have a job at all.' She shrugged her shoulders. 'They are all corrupt and out to make money for themselves, even at the expense of their junior staff. It happened to other girls and they just accepted the situation and worked for half of their proper pay. I was too proud to do that, so I quit.'

'There must be someone to whom you can complain,' said Peter indignantly.

'This is Russia. You can't complain.'

They had reached the hotel. It was starting to snow as Natasha had predicted. Peter got out of the car. 'So when

Ticket to Tallinn

do I see you?'

'Vladimir and I will come to pick you up at seven o'clock. Is that all right?'

'Fine.'

Peter walked up the concrete steps to the thick glass entrance doors of the hotel. He opened them and was blasted by hot air from the central heating system, which banished the outside chill. He walked over towards the reception desk, and, as he did so, a man wearing a shabby suit and a brown fur hat walked up to him.

'Do you want to change money? I can give you a good rate.' The man looked up at him with narrowed eyes and slowly patted his coat pocket.

'No, thank you.'

'Are you sure?' Peter inhaled the familiar smell of bad breath, now mingled with stale tobacco.

'Quite sure, thank you.'

The man moved away, and, as he did so, Peter noticed two men watching him closely. They were half hidden behind a large pillar and as he looked up they immediately turned away. Peter walked towards the reception desk feeling distinctly uneasy.

'Can I have my key, please? It is room 624.'

'You will find the key with the concierge on the sixth floor.' The bad-tempered, middle-aged woman who made this statement immediately made him feel foolish. 'I believe you left the key with her like the other guests.'

'Yes.'

'Then you will collect it from her.'

The contrast with the friendly Natasha could not have been greater. Peter was about to protest at her rudeness

This is Roger

but checked himself. It would achieve nothing.

He moved away towards the lift. The two men were still watching him. Their fat, fleshy, expressionless faces betrayed no emotion whatsoever. Three of the six hotel lifts were out of order. Travelling to a bedroom became a lengthy and tedious business and the hotel appeared to have no stairs. When Peter finally reached the sixth floor, he noticed that the concierge who sat at a little table just beyond the lifts was different to the one to whom he had given his key that morning.

'Room 624, please.'

'Uh?'

'Six-two-four,' said Peter, articulating each word.

'Message for you,' said the woman as she reached for the key. When she had handed it to him she unlocked a drawer and handed Peter a folded piece of paper. Peter unfolded it and read, 'Roger will ring at six'.

'I think there is a mistake. I don't know a "Roger".'

The woman muttered something moodily in Russian which clearly meant that she had no idea or interest in what he was talking about. She picked up a half-knitted sweater, seated herself in her chair, and without looking up at him began to knit. Sensing that there was absolutely no point in engaging her in any further conversation, Peter went to his room and unlocked the door. Once inside he made a quick check of his belongings to see whether they had been disturbed or stolen. Everything seemed to be in order. Then he glanced at his watch. It was a quarter to six. At precisely six o'clock the phone rang.

'Hello.'

17

Ticket to Tallinn

'Hello,' said a muffled voice. The line was cracking and the speaker seemed a long way away. 'This is Roger. Do you understand? This is Roger.'

'I think that there is some mistake. I don't know anyone called Roger. I think you are speaking to the wrong person.'

'No,' came the reply. There seemed to be another person muttering something in the background. 'No, you are the right person. I repeat, this is Roger.'

'Sorry,' said Peter abruptly. 'Wrong number.' He replaced the receiver and started to take a bath.

He picked two cockroaches out of the bath before turning on the hot tap. The water was only just warm. When the bath was full he undressed and started to get in. The telephone rang. He put a towel around his waist and lifted the receiver.

'Hello, this is Roger.'

'I have told you that you have the wrong number. Who do you wish to speak to?'

'Mister Peter.' On hearing this Peter shivered in alarm. Something very strange was going on.

'My name is Peter but I don't know a "Roger".'

'You are in room 624?'

'Yes.'

'This is Roger.'

Peter replaced the receiver. He wanted to get into his bath before the water was completely cold. No sooner was he in than the telephone rang again. This time there was no hesitating. He picked up the receiver and shouted, 'Sod off, Roger!' He left the receiver off the hook and resumed his bath.

Chapter 2
So sorry, Mister Peter

'I never realised that an English gentleman could be so rude,' said Natasha when they met in the hotel lobby. 'What did you say to me, "sod off"?'

Peter looked at her in embarrassed amazement. 'But I had no idea ...'

'Well, you should be more careful. We may have our faults in Russia, but we don't talk to our friends like that, even if they do in England.' She was clearly upset and so was Vladimir, who was standing protectively by her side. 'After all, we are taking you to the circus. I don't see any reason why you should behave so rudely.'

'Please, listen to me,' said Peter, horrified at what had happened. He hurriedly explained about the mysterious telephone calls which had been made to his hotel room, and the explanation immediately satisfied them. However, it left Natasha looking distinctly worried. 'Someone is after you for some reason,' she whispered.

'Those two guys over there are taking an unusual interest in me,' he said, indicating the two men who had been staring at him when he had first arrived at the hotel. 'They have been following every move I make.'

'Gooks,' said Vladimir.

'What?'

'KGB. Stands out a mile. Come, let's go.'

He propelled them towards the hotel doors and Peter

Ticket to Tallinn

felt the eyes of the two 'gooks' following them.

Seated in the Volvo, Natasha apologised for her outburst and then introduced Vladimir. He was over two metres tall, softly spoken and with blonde curly hair. He was dressed in jeans and a chunky brown sweater.

'Vladimir's a Christian,' said Natasha. 'He is trying to convert me but I am not ready to be converted yet.'

'You will be soon,' said Vladimir, gently kissing her. 'Are you a Christian?' he asked Peter, staring hard at him with large, penetrating blue eyes.

'Not really.'

'Why not? You should be.'

'Stop it, Vladimir,' said Natasha. 'Leave him alone.' She turned to Peter. 'Vladimir is a "born again" Christian,' she explained. 'He has had a dramatic religious experience and cannot stop talking about it. Luckily, nobody calls him mad and locks him up, as they would have done a few years ago.'

Peter changed the subject by asking who Vladimir thought Roger was, and what he wanted.

'I don't know,' said Vladimir. 'Are you sure that you don't know a "Roger"?'

'Quite sure.'

'Well, in that case, whoever rang you must have been using a code which he thought you understood.'

'Couldn't the message have been meant for a previous occupant of my room?'

'Yes, that's possible. You will soon find out. If he keeps trying to contact you, then the message will be for you.'

'But this is my first visit to the USSR. I have no

So sorry, Mister Peter

contacts here. I have never had any hand in any undercover activities.'

Vladimir smiled. 'Maybe someone thinks that you can be of use to them.' Noticing Peter's worried expression he added, 'But don't worry, they are so stupid that it is usually quite easy to outwit them.'

They had now reached the suburbs and Natasha was explaining that they were heading for a new circus hall which had only recently been constructed. 'You see how popular the circus is,' she said. 'Where else in Europe are they building circus halls?'

The Volvo slowed to a stop outside a modern, circular, metal and concrete construction which housed the circus. Crowds of people were hurrying towards the doors. 'It's always full,' Natasha continued.

Galina had booked good seats but as soon as they were seated Vladimir started to talk once more to Peter about religion.

'I cannot understand why you reject it,' he said. 'For me it is my life.'

'It is for many others in the world, but I am afraid that it is not for me.'

Peter turned to Natasha but Vladimir persisted. 'Even if you are not a practising Christian, will you do a Christian act for me?'

'It depends what it is.'

'I have an eight-hundred-page manuscript, a book written in Russian which discusses all the religious philosophies and beliefs which are active or which have lain dormant in the Soviet Union. I feel very strongly that the English-speaking world should be made aware

Ticket to Tallinn

of it. Will you take it to the West and try to have it translated and published for me?'

'Leave Peter alone, Vladimir,' interjected Natasha. 'He has come here to enjoy himself.'

Vladimir said nothing but continued to fix Peter with his penetrating, bright blue eyes.

'Will you?'

'Well, I don't really ...'

'Forget it,' said Natasha gripping his arm tightly. 'The circus is about to begin. You can discuss it later.'

Vladimir was continuing to whisper, 'Will you?', when with a great crash the orchestra started to play the march from *The Entry of the Gladiators*, and the grand parade of the circus performers began.

Peter's mind was reeling long before the interval. The colour, the sounds and sensations which emanated from the slickest and most professional of performances intoxicated him. Act followed spectacular act. The circus followed traditions which had long since died out in Western Europe, yet they were performed with such skill that they seemed totally fresh and modern. The triple somersaults performed by the trapeze artists, the spectacular jugglers, the bears on bicycles, the seals blowing trumpets – none of these acts were new. But Peter was left speechless by the manner in which one polished and perfectly executed performance followed another. When the black panther jumped over the lion tamer and lay down with the tigers, who themselves were nestling up to the lions, he could not believe what he saw. 'Fantastic,' he kept repeating to Natasha. 'Quite fantastic.'

So sorry, Mister Peter

Ticket to Tallinn

It was during that first interval when they were queuing for tea and cake, that Peter was abruptly reminded of the disquieting events which had occurred earlier that day. The queue round the counter selling tea suddenly turned into a mass of pushing people who sensed that the circus would shortly be re-starting. Peter, who had just bought a cup of tea, was turning to speak to Vladimir when someone stumbled against him and spilt his tea down the side of his jacket.

Immediately a hand was placed on his arm and he looked up into the face of a total stranger who said quite distinctly, 'I am so sorry, Mister Peter.'

Peter was about to speak to him when the man disappeared into the crowd. He looked hastily around for Vladimir and Natasha and saw that they had been separated from him by the milling crowd and had not seen what had happened to him. He pushed his way towards them.

'What happened?' asked Natasha, looking down in concern at his stained jacket.

'I was deliberately pushed by a man who called me "Mister Peter".'

Both Vladimir and Natasha looked at Peter in alarm.

'He called you "Mister Peter"?'

'Yes, I had just bought my tea when I felt someone push me from behind. When I turned round a perfect stranger apologised to me, and called me "Mister Peter".'

'This is getting serious,' said Vladimir. 'It is now certain that someone is trying to get to you. Have you any idea why?'

So sorry, Mister Peter

'No, none at all.'

'What did he do after he had spoken to you?' asked Natasha.

'He immediately disappeared in the crowd.'

'He must have been trying to make sure that the next time you received a telephone call from Roger you would not put the receiver down.'

A bell rang loudly behind them.

'Come, we must return to our seats,' said Natasha. 'As Vladimir said, this interference by Roger is becoming serious.'

The second half of the circus was even more spectacular than the first, but Peter enjoyed it far less. The unnerving encounter with the man who called him Mister Peter was all he could think about. Not even the illusionist who not only sawed a woman in half but also sliced her into quarters could take his mind off his recent encounter with the stranger.

'You must change your room,' said Natasha firmly as they were driving back to Peter's hotel. 'I will insist that they move you. We will say your room is too noisy. We must try to ensure that the person calling himself Roger doesn't bother you again.'

'But it's not a coincidence,' said Peter slowly. 'For reasons that I can't begin to understand, he clearly wants to speak to me.'

'It may be best if you let him,' said Vladimir. 'Then at least you will know what he wants with you.'

Against Natasha's advice, Peter decided to remain in his room, but as the lift ascended to the sixth floor he wondered whether he should do so. He looked anxiously at the careworn face of the concierge as she searched for the key to his room, fearful that she might give him another note from Roger. But she just glowered at him and then looked away as she handed over the long brass key to room 624. He hesitated before inserting the key in the lock, uncertain whether someone might already be inside the room waiting for him. He slowly turned the key, opened the door and entered.

He switched on the light. There was no one there. He thankfully took an uninterrupted bath and prepared to get into bed. Just before he did so he took a look at his stained jacket and decided to wipe it with a damp cloth. He started to take everything out of his pockets. As he did so he felt an envelope. That's strange, he thought, as he removed it from his pocket. He turned it over. There were two words written on the envelope – 'From Roger'.

He fingered it carefully in case it was a letter bomb. Feeling nothing bulky inside it, he opened it and unfolded a letter.

'Dear Mister Peter,' it began. 'As I have been unable to contact you on the telephone, I had to find an excuse to get this to you without other people seeing either me or this letter.

'I need to see you very urgently. I believe that you have two more days in the USSR and that your last full day is Saturday. Your friends will ask what you would like to do on your last day. Could you please say that you would like to visit the Zagorsk monastery, which is about forty kilometres from Moscow. I am sure they will agree to take you there. When you arrive, ask to be taken to the former Imperial Chapel. I will meet you there.

So sorry, Mister Peter

'Please do not tell *anyone* that you have received this letter, or that you have had any further contact with me. Believe me when I say that everything is for the good. Trust me. I, and others, need your help very badly. When you have read this letter – destroy it. Roger.'

Peter read the letter again. Then he tore it into small pieces and flushed it down the lavatory. Clearly, whoever had written it knew a great deal about him and his movements. What the writer did not know was that Victor had already suggested that on his last day he ought to visit Red Square and the Kremlin. Peter, not unnaturally, had replied that he would be delighted to do so. Don't get involved, he thought to himself. Don't get involved with people and forces which you know nothing about. Ignore the letter and forget it. At that moment the telephone rang. Even before he picked up the receiver he knew who it was.

'Hello, this is Roger,' a distant voice began. 'I look forward to meeting you – please come as arranged.'

Peter heard a faint click on the line. He had read enough spy stories to know the sound of a tapped telephone.

'I'll be there,' he said impulsively. 'Goodbye.'

He replaced the receiver and looked at his reflection in the mirror by his bed. 'What are you doing, you fool?' he said out loud. 'What are you letting yourself in for?'

But the next morning when he woke up with a bad taste in his mouth from indifferent food and a foul bedroom atmosphere he felt no remorse for his impulsive action. The frustrations and lack of achievements of the visit had made him reckless.

The next day was full of more frustration. Victor was even more elusive concerning the proposed visit of the environmentalists. He said that he would refer it to higher authority. That he would approach the relevant sources. That he would apply 'appropriate pressure'. All this amounted to was total inaction. So when, at the end of the day, Victor asked him to suggest a time when he should pick him up to take him to the Kremlin, he replied coolly, 'I'd rather not go.'

'What!' exclaimed Victor, raising his bushy eyebrows in surprise. 'You have something better to do? That I cannot believe. You must visit Red Square and see the Kremlin.'

'If you don't mind, I would rather visit the Zagorsk monastery. I was told in England that I must try to go there if I had a chance. Apparently the architecture is stunning and I have always had a great interest in Russian religious architecture.' Peter reflected on how coolly he could lie.

'Stunning? What does stunning mean?'

'Very remarkable – most unusual – unique. Do you think you can arrange it?'

'But,' began Victor, 'it is more than forty –'

Galina cut him off. 'Of course, Mister Peter, I will take you even if Victor doesn't want to come. Natasha will come with us as well.'

Victor scratched his nose. 'All right, Galina, you take Peter, and I will stay behind to arrange his farewell party. After all, he is my new business colleague, and business parties are very new to us in Russia.'

Peter was relieved that Victor was not going to come

So sorry, Mister Peter

with them. He felt that his newly acquired business colleague could not be trusted to handle Roger's affairs.

Victor's hairy hand encompassed the vodka bottle and soon the frustrations of the day were dispelled in an alcoholic glow which left Peter gloomy; as far as the relationship between the COP and ICEP was concerned, nothing had been achieved.

Saturday dawned, grey, windy and wet. Some of the rain was already turning into soft snow, which melted as soon as it made contact with the wet roads and pavements. The wind blew icy cold, a bleak breath of Siberian grimness.

Galina and Natasha were waiting for Peter in the lobby of the hotel when he arrived, a little after the agreed time of nine o'clock. The two 'gooks' stared dispassionately as he embraced first Galina and then her lovely daughter. 'I'm sorry I'm late. I have been waiting ages for the lift.'

Natasha took his arm and pulled him close towards her in front of the two KGB men. 'Don't worry, we haven't been here long and our friends over there have been entertaining us.' She nodded in the direction of the 'gooks', who continued to stare at them.

'Stop it,' whispered Galina to Natasha. 'You'll get us all into trouble if you talk like that.'

Natasha gave her a look of contempt. 'Oh, Mama, they are so stupid. Why worry about them?'

They stepped out into the freezing wind and hurried towards the parked Volvo. As they drove on to the main road, the two KGB watchers bundled themselves into a black car and began to follow them.

'Oh hell, how boring, they are going to tail us,' said Natasha who had spotted them in the Volvo's wing mirror. She immediately said something to the driver in Russian.

'Natasha has told him to lose them,' explained Galina to Peter. 'We don't want them spoiling our day.'

'But why are they bothering about us?' asked Peter, who was anxiously thinking about his real motive for wanting to be taken to the monastery.

'Goodness knows. Russia may have changed, but it hasn't changed that much, and in some places a foreigner is still suspected of being up to no good. Luckily, we have a good driver. I promise you that he will have shaken them off in ten minutes.'

And he did, with a couple of quick turns down two side streets and a sharp reversal down another which was intended for one-way traffic only. But Peter's anxiety continued to increase and his early morning bravado quickly evaporated.

As they sped along a highway heading north out of Moscow, Galina took great delight in pointing out establishments which were supposed to be 'secret', although every Muscovite knew exactly what really went on behind their austere walls.

'That one manufactures special rockets for our ambitious space programme,' she said, pointing to a large red-brick building which could have manufactured anything. 'And that one is very secret,' she cried out with a laugh as she pointed out another featureless, brick-red building. 'That is where some of our chemical

So sorry, Mister Peter

weapons are made.'

'What is officially supposed to be made there?' asked Peter.

'Razor blades,' came the surprising reply.

They sped on through flat agricultural land, dotted here and there with huge buildings built to store grain from the cooperative farms situated in the area. In the snow the grey concrete constructions looked like giant seagoing tankers sailing on a sea of brown mud.

Thirty minutes later Natasha suddenly pointed excitedly to her right. 'Look, there are the towers of the monastery. See, the sun has come out to light them up for you. Aren't they beautiful?'

The sun had appeared momentarily from behind menacing dark clouds; it lit up with a watery light the brilliant blue and gold onion-shaped domes of the churches and chapels which dominated the ancient monastery.

'What a contrast to all that we have seen since we left Moscow,' said Peter. 'Out of the darkness and into the light.'

A few minutes later they were rattling along twisting cobblestone roads and then up to the great gates of the monastery, which were set in a high white wall which encircled the site. There were few people about. The miserable weather had kept people in their flats and houses, fighting for warmth.

'How did this monastery manage to survive the last seventy years of communism?' Peter asked. 'I thought that nearly all the churches and sacred buildings were razed to the ground.'

'Many were,' Natasha answered, 'but luckily someone had the foresight to preserve Zagorsk. It was a museum until two years ago and then, in the new political climate, novice monks were once again allowed to enrol and pursue their religious studies.'

They left the drive to park the car and walked up to the massive medieval wooden gates. One of the gates had a small entrance door set in the middle of it, and, as it was open, they walked through. A uniformed guide met them and led them over to an office where two armed military men were seated behind a high wooden desk which stretched across the whole width of a small room. The men looked unsmilingly at Peter as Galina produced her identity card and Natasha did the same.

'Show them your passport, please,' Galina said to Peter.

Peter took out his *Laissez Passer* which his status with the ICEP, an organisation with links to the United Nations, allowed him to carry. It was a valuable document, because it not only carried with it the privilege of diplomatic immunity, but it also enabled him to pass freely through custom checks around the world.

The military men's eyes narrowed when they saw it and they asked Galina a few abrupt questions which she answered to their apparent satisfaction.

'They will keep your *Laissez Passer* while we are inside the monastery,' said Galina, 'but you will be given it back when we leave.'

'Do I have to leave it with them?'

'I'm afraid so, but there is nothing unusual in that. All

So sorry, Mister Peter

Ticket to Tallinn

foreigners have to leave their passports here.'

Peter reluctantly handed over the precious document, and they left the office without Peter having been asked a single question by the two grimfaced figures behind the desk.

The monastery buildings were magnificent. Built between the fourteenth and nineteenth centuries, they comprised churches and chapels in different architectural styles; without exception, they were topped with the huge onion-shaped domes peculiar to the Orthodox religion. Some were made of gleaming golden brass, others were painted bright blue or striped with red and white diagonal stripes.

The novice monks had been allowed to occupy the quarters which had originally been constructed for their use centuries earlier. It was there that the three visitors began their tour under the close supervision of their appointed guide.

'Does he have to stay with us?' Peter whispered to Natasha.

'It will be very difficult to give him the slip,' she replied. 'They stick to foreign visitors like – how do you say it in English? – like a leech.'

Peter wondered how Roger was going to manage to contact him with a 'leech' by his side. However, I suppose that's his problem, not mine, he thought to himself.

Two young novice monks, who looked as though they were still in their teens, attached themselves to them as they entered the monks' living quarters. They took them around the sparsely furnished, austere building and

So sorry, Mister Peter

explained their daily routine.

'Is it popular among youngsters to become a novice monk?' Peter asked one of them.

'Since *"glasnost"*, there has been a flood of applicants,' the monk replied. 'There are over five hundred applicants on this monastery's waiting-list alone.'

After the tour of monks' quarters they were led from one chapel to another; without exception they were of breathtaking beauty. They were full of golden ornaments and precious icons which were cared for lovingly by an army of aged women. In some of the chapels, services were taking place and in answer to Peter's question the monks replied that a service was held somewhere in the monastery every hour of the day and night, seven days a week.

'The extent of the religious revival in the USSR should not be underestimated,' one of the monks remarked solemnly to Peter. 'Officially discouraged for so many years from even entering a church, many people today have an unsatisfied longing for the peace and beauty of our services.'

'But the very best we have reserved for you until the last,' the other monk interjected. 'We will conclude our tour with a visit to the Imperial Chapel. I can assure you that you will be very impressed.'

Peter tensed with a faint emotion of fear. He had been so absorbed by the history of the monastery and its magnificent architecture that he had quite forgotten about Roger and that if it hadn't been for Roger, he would never have come here at all.

35

Chapter 3
Guard it with your Life

'The Imperial Chapel, where the last Tsar was crowned and where the royal family made their devotions.' The monk who said this spread his arms out in front of him.

'Isn't it beautiful?' Natasha whispered to Peter.

Peter was only half listening. His eyes had taken in the dazzling beauty of his surroundings, but his mind was on other matters of more immediate importance. 'Yes, very,' he replied as he walked away from her to the centre of the chapel. He looked round about him. Apart from an old cleaning woman who was polishing the altar candlesticks, the chapel was empty. He walked back towards his companions.

'Aren't you impressed, Mister Peter?'

'I'm very impressed,' mumbled Peter, forcing himself to concentrate on the one hundred and eight icons which were lined up row upon row behind the high altar, and which one of the monks was describing to the visitors.

'Look up at the ceiling,' said Galina. 'It's so beautiful.' And indeed it was, with its brightly painted biblical scenes depicting pictures of saints and angels and their heroic deeds. The other monk explained that it had recently been restored – a further example of the change in the authorities' attitude towards religion.

'The icons date from the twelfth century and were painted with … '

Peter moved away from the group and towards the

Guard it with your Life

altar where he could see the icons more closely. 'They are very beautiful,' he exclaimed.

He was suddenly conscious of the old lady who was cleaning the altar brass. She was dressed entirely in black, and a black shawl was draped over her head, obscuring her features. She was slowly walking towards him, a candlestick in either hand, and when she was only a few paces away from him she turned to place the candlesticks on the altar. As she did so she tripped and fell to the floor. Peter bent down to help her to her feet, and as he did so, she gripped his arm tightly, whispered the one word 'Roger', and pressed a small packet into his hand.

Peter could hear the cries of alarm of the others who were running towards them, but by the time they had reached the altar he had helped the old woman to her feet, and slipped the packet into his jacket pocket.

Galina went up to her to enquire if she was all right, but she merely muttered something in Russian and turned away to continue her work.

Peter breathed a sigh of relief that nobody had seen what passed between the old lady and himself. The monk continued to expound on the glories of the icons and Peter, freed from the worry of what might happen to him in the Imperial Chapel, was now able to take an interest in what he was saying.

'This icon will be of particular interest to the English visitor,' the monk intoned, looking hard at Peter. 'It was presented to the Imperial Chapel by an Englishman called Roger Coverdale in 1893. His ancestor had been given the icon by the then Tsar of Russia in 1710, in

Ticket to Tallinn

gratitude for some deed that he performed for the Imperial family in Tallinn, Estonia.'

Peter tensed. Was this monk trying to pass a message to him?

'What was the deed?' he asked.

'We don't know exactly what he did. What we do know was that in some way it served the cause of Estonian freedom.'

'That is a very topical subject at the moment.'

'Quite right,' said the monk. 'I am sure that some Estonians would like to find someone today to perform a similar act.'

'I don't think that we should involve our guest in our domestic politics,' said Galina. 'Please explain the significance of that plaque over there.'

They moved towards the spot where the last and late Tsar was crowned and the monk began another lengthy explanation. Peter was no longer listening. He was studying the man closely, convinced that the monk was aware that he had been given the small packet, and that it had something to do with the next stage of his journey to Tallinn. But was this mild-mannered monk Roger? He put his hand into his jacket pocket and felt the little packet. All he wanted to do now was to return to his hotel and find out what it contained. As though she had mysteriously read his thoughts Galina suddenly looked at her watch and exclaimed, 'Goodness, is that the time? We have to hurry back to Moscow for Peter's farewell party. Unless we leave soon we will be late.'

She turned to the monk and spoke to him in Russian. He gave a slight bow.

Guard it with your Life

'I hope that you enjoyed your visit,' he said, shaking Peter by the hand.

'I found it most enjoyable and was particularly interested in your remarks about the history of the Englishman and the icon.'

The monk looked at him and smiled. 'I thought you would be,' he said. 'May God be with you.'

Peter was now firmly convinced that the monk either knew or was Roger. He was about to say something further but the man turned away and started to speak to Galina and Natasha in Russian. They walked over to the main door and said farewell to the two monks.

'I must say that was the most interesting part of my visit to Moscow so far. Thank you so much for altering the programme to allow me to come here. I have enjoyed it.' Peter spoke mechanically without realising what he was saying. The excitements of the past fifteen minutes were uppermost in his mind.

'We mustn't forget to collect your passport,' said Galina. 'Let's go and get it now.'

It was snowing hard and the temperature had dropped still further as they made their way back to the office where Peter had left his *Laissez Passer*. Peter walked up to the desk and was immediately handed the light blue document which gave him such valuable diplomatic immunity. He put it in his jacket pocket and they walked out of the monastery towards their waiting vehicle.

'I had no idea it was getting so late,' said Galina, hurrying them along. 'Victor won't be pleased if we're late. I know he's arranged something special for you.'

'I would be much happier if I wasn't leaving having

Ticket to Tallinn

achieved nothing,' Peter said to her. 'Parties, monasteries and the circus are all very well, but I didn't come here as a tourist!'

'Patience, patience,' said Natasha who had been quiet for a long time. She patted him on the arm. 'I am sure that you will accomplish a great deal very shortly.'

Peter looked at her thoughtfully. Did she know something? Was she involved with Roger too? Then he remembered their earlier conversation when she had implied that she was hoping to obtain something from him.

'What's the matter?' she asked with concern, sensing his sudden change in attitude. 'Did I say something wrong?'

'Nothing at all.'

She took his arm and hurried him towards the car. 'Everything will be all right,' she whispered softly.

Galina chatted non-stop all the way back to Moscow. Once or twice Peter felt for the little package in his pocket to make quite certain that it was still there. Was it his imagination, or was Natasha behaving more warmly towards him? They reached Peter's hotel.

'You have time for a very quick wash,' Natasha said. 'We will wait for you here, but please don't take more than twenty minutes.'

Peter hurried towards the hotel entrance. He was too preoccupied to check whether the two KGB minders were still there and for once the lift appeared promptly and whisked him up to the sixth floor. When he arrived the concierge was not there.

'Damn. Where's my key? he said to himself as he

Guard it with your Life

began to rummage in the drawer where she kept the room keys. He picked up each key in turn. Not one was numbered 624.

'Where's my key?' he shouted.

A hand was placed on his shoulder and he turned round to face the concierge. 'Here,' she said, holding the key up in front of his face. 'Why can't you wait until I come?'

'Because I'm in a hurry, that's why. And what are you doing with my key? Have you been in my room?'

She replied in Russian, gave him the key and turned away. He cursed her under his breath and hurried towards his room, certain that she was watching him.

Once inside his room he checked all his belongings. Everything seemed to be in order, so he sat down on his bed and pulled out the mysterious package. It was wrapped in brown paper which was tied with thin string. When he had untied it he uncovered a note and a roll of miniature film.

'Mister Peter,' the note began. 'You are entrusted with this very important film. Please take it to London and when you get there, telephone 071 543 6622. Say that you have come from Roger. When you reach Tallinn, please go to the Maiasmokk café in Pikk Street in the old city. Tourists visit Maiasmokk (the Sweet Tooth Café) and you will not be out of place there. Someone will make contact with you.

'Destroy this note immediately you have read it. The film is very valuable. Guard it with your life. I advise you to roll up your left shirt sleeve very tightly and roll the film up with it. You should be able to travel with it

Ticket to Tallinn

quite safely, with the minimum risk of detection. It cannot be identified by those machines you pass through at the airport, nor harmed by them in any way. Our gratitude knows no limits. Roger.'

Peter wrote the telephone number backwards on the back of one of his visitor's cards and placed it in his wallet. Then he took off his jacket and rolled up both his sleeves. In the left-hand sleeve he carefully inserted the roll of film. He was just about to go to the lavatory to dispose of the letter when there was a loud knock on the door. Stuffing the letter into his trouser pocket he went to the door and opened it. It was the concierge.

'Can I come in?'

'Sorry.'

'Are you leaving tonight?'

'Yes.'

'Where are you going to?'

'It is no concern of yours. Kindly leave me alone. I'm in a hurry.'

She leaned towards him. 'Would you like to change some money? I will give you a good rate.'

'No thanks, I wouldn't. Please leave me alone.' He pushed her roughly away from him. 'If you bother me again I will report you to the security men downstairs.'

Seeing that she was getting nowhere she abruptly switched to Russian and shouted abuse at him. Bedroom doors opened and anxious faces peered out.

The last thing I want is unwelcome publicity, Peter thought to himself. With a great shove, he pushed her away from the door, slammed it shut and bolted it.

He looked at his watch and saw to his horror that it

was already twenty-five minutes since he had left Natasha and Galina sitting in the car outside the hotel. He hastily brushed his hair and adjusted his tie. His suitcase was already packed and he picked it up together with his briefcase. As he left his room, he noted with great relief that the concierge was not behind her desk. 'No doubt trying to cheat some other helpless foreigner,' he muttered to himself. This time the lift reverted to its former practice and he impatiently spent five minutes waiting for it to come. It descended slowly, stopping at every floor on the way and when he reached the hotel lobby he immediately spotted Natasha and Galina.

'We had to come inside. We were so cold in the car. Why were you so long?' Natasha looked nervous.

'I'm sorry, the concierge took the key and then tried to make me change my money at a black market rate.'

'Quick! Come to the desk and check out.'

Galina hustled Peter towards the reception desk. The account was being paid by COP in roubles, and as this had been arranged in advance, all that was required from Peter was a signature.

He studied the figures on the bill. 'Is it correct?' he asked Galina. She nodded and he signed the account. They hurried out of the hotel and were soon speeding towards the outskirts of Moscow. Victor had sensibly chosen a restaurant as near to the airport as possible, and twenty minutes later, they slowed to a stop outside a grey, featureless, concrete building which housed one of the few state restaurants of quality. Galina was excited. 'Only the successful can afford to eat here,' she said. 'It is very expensive. I don't know where Victor finds the money but he always seems to get it from somewhere.'

As they entered the restaurant Peter saw that about thirty tables had been placed around a central dance floor. The room was brightly lit and the dazzling lights were concentrated on large wall paintings showing male and female workers bringing in the harvest. It seemed to be a strange décor for a fashionable restaurant, but was intended as a forcible reminder to the affluent diners that they should have no illusions that they were still living under communism. Their entrance was immediately spotted by Victor, who jumped up from the table where he was seated with two other COP officials, and hurried over towards them.

'What's kept you?' he asked Galina. 'I thought that maybe our English friend had decided to become a novice monk.'

'It's my fault, Victor,' said Peter. 'I was unfortunately delayed at the hotel by the attentions of a concierge.'

'Was she pretty? Was she worth it?' Victor asked with a great guffaw of laughter. 'If she was worth it then I forgive your lateness.'

'Unfortunately not. She was trying to get hold of some of my foreign currency by offering me a very special rate of exchange.'

'Not an uncommon practice. But you've checked out?'

'Yes.'

'Okay, now let's see. Your plane leaves at eleven fifteen. It's now twenty-five minutes past seven. So we should leave here in two hours' time.' He led them over to a table. 'The food here is excellent. The vodka is in

Guard it with your Life

my bag. Let us now enjoy ourselves. May I introduce my two good friends from COP, Ivan and Valentina.'

One hour and twenty minutes later, after half a bottle of vodka and a satisfying meal, Peter was feeling more like a sleep than a dance. But a band had struck up lively music and Natasha was whispering, 'Go on, Mister Peter, dance with my mother.'

It was hot in the room, and as Peter rose unsteadily to his feet and took Galina by the hand, his head began to spin with the effects of the alcohol.

'It would give the Englishman great pleasure if he could have this dance with the gorgeous Galina,' he said in a slightly drunken drawl.

Galina laughed. 'The Englishman's wish is granted,' she replied. 'Galina would be delighted!'

The music was noisy and lively, and, in spite of his head, Peter immediately launched them into a vigorous dance. Conversation was impossible. He was a good dancer and so was Galina and as they twirled around the dance floor the other dancers broke off to watch them and clap in time to the beat of the band.

'Enough, enough,' cried Galina suddenly.

'Just one more,' cried the excited Peter, who was by now red in the face and very hot indeed. Exhilarated both by the vodka and his exertions, he had forgotten that he would soon be heading for the airport.

Eventually, Peter persuaded Galina to have just one more dance with him, to the delight of the spectators; when it was over, he reached into his pocket to pull out his handkerchief and mop his forehead. As he did so, a piece of paper fluttered to the floor.

'That's it. I'm finished.'

'You're finished! What about me?' Galina exclaimed, panting for breath. 'Aren't you going to have at least one dance with Natasha?'

'No, no, I haven't got any energy left.'

Natasha, however, was already by his side. 'You will have one dance with me, Mister Peter,' she commanded. There was a gleam in her eye which clearly stated that she wasn't prepared to take 'no' for an answer.

'But have I time?' Peter protested. 'Shouldn't we be getting ready to go to the airport?'

'We have still got time.' There was no stopping her. She was determined to have her dance with him.

Once on the dance floor she propelled him away from the band, to a place where they couldn't be seen by their companions at the dining table.

'I think this belongs to you,' she said holding a piece of paper in front of him. 'Why did you put it in your pocket when you were told to destroy it? Why didn't you do what you were asked to do?'

'You know?'

'Of course I do. Oh, dear God, why did we have to pick someone so unreliable?'

'But I don't understand.'

She gave him a scornful glance. 'No, I don't suppose that you do, but do you understand what you did? When you pulled your handkerchief out of your pocket this precious letter fell to the floor. Thank goodness I saw what happened and managed to pick it up before anyone else did. If someone had picked it up and read it, it would have wrecked everything.'

'But why are you involved in all this?'

She ignored the question. 'Where's the film?' she whispered anxiously.

'Where I was instructed to put it.'

'Is it still there?'

'Listen,' Peter said coldly. 'I didn't ask to do your dirty work for you. I didn't volunteer.'

'No, but you told Roger you would help us.' She suddenly became aware of the fact that some people were looking at them with interest. 'Quickly, start to dance with me. People are staring at us. We can't stand here talking to each other.' He led her on to the dance floor and they started to dance.

'What are you going to do with the letter?' he asked.

'Destroy it, of course.'

'Natasha, will you please tell me exactly what is going on?'

Whether she was intending to answer that question he never found out because a hairy hand was suddenly placed firmly on his shoulder, forcing him to stop dancing.

'Are you two having an argument or something?' Victor had walked on to the dance floor.

'No, no,' said Natasha hurriedly,' I was just teaching Mister Peter some useful Russian phrases.'

'Well, he didn't seem to be enjoying the lesson very much,' said Victor, looking with interest from one to the other. 'Come, it is time for us to go.'

Peter was suddenly conscious that everyone in the room seemed to be staring at them. The heated conversation with the pretty Natasha had given the other

Guard it with your Life

diners something to talk about. The last thing he wanted to do at this stage was to draw unwanted attention to himself. As he walked back to their table he remembered that at the circus Vladimir had mentioned something about taking a manuscript out of the country for him. He was on the point of starting to say something about it to Natasha but checked himself. The film and the instructions from Roger had given him quite enough to worry about without getting himself into more difficulty by carrying additional illicit material out of the country. The fact that I have diplomatic immunity seems to be the reason why I am being used in this way, he thought. The chances of my being stopped and searched are much less than if I had an ordinary EEC or British passport.

'You are very quiet, Mister Peter,' said Victor as they all drove towards the airport. 'Was the meal and the vodka not to your liking?'

'No, not at all. I can't thank you enough for making my stay such a pleasant one. I only wish that I could have reached agreement with you on the international visit.'

'But what of our other agreement?'

'As I told you, I will write to you.'

'Soon?'

'As soon as I return.'

'And send your order.'

'That's what we agreed.'

They had reached the outskirts of the airport and the driver was soon looking desperately for a place to park.

'The airport seems very busy even though it is late.'

'There is not enough parking space. The traffic has

expanded but the airport has not grown at all.'

The truth of this remark was even more evident when they were inside the airport. The limited floor space was swarming with travellers and the queues for the check-in desk and passport control were enormous.

'I shall see you through,' said Victor confidently. 'Can I have your ticket and your *Laissez Passer*?' Peter handed them over and Victor walked over to the far side of the airport and knocked on an unmarked door. It was opened and he disappeared inside.

'Where's he gone?' Peter asked Natasha.

'He has influence here,' she replied. She had said nothing to him in the car and was clearly still angry that he had not destroyed the letter from Roger as instructed.

Galina had moved over to a paper stall to buy a magazine and for a few moments they were on their own.

'I'm sorry about what happened. I won't let you down again.'

She looked at him and placed a hand on his arm. 'Thank you. Please do your best. It is very important to a great many people who are depending on you. But don't talk to me any more about this. This place is dangerous and very unsafe.' She gave his arm a slight squeeze. There were a hundred questions he would very much have loved to ask her. How was it that she was involved? Did her mother know? Did Vladimir? Who was Roger and was he the monk? How had the cleaning woman been involved? And most vital of all, what was on the micro film? He was anxious to know the answers to all these questions, but he held his tongue.

Guard it with your Life

'Did you find what you were looking for?' he asked Galina when she returned.

'Yes, it's for you,' she said, holding out a booklet. 'A guide to Tallinn.'

'That's very kind of you.'

'It will help you find your way to the Sweet Tooth Café.'

Peter stared at her in amazement. One of his questions had been answered. Galina knew.

He could see Victor out of the corner of his eye, striding towards them, and quickly changed the topic of conversation.

'Will it be as cold as this in Tallinn?' he asked.

'Oh no. Tallinn will be warmer. They don't have hard winters like we do in Moscow.'

'It's all settled,' said Victor triumphantly. 'That man over there will see to everything.' He handed Peter his ticket and *Laissez Passer*. 'So now we must say goodbye.'

He shook hands warmly with Victor and embraced Galina and Natasha.

'Write to me. Please write.'

'Of course I will, Natasha. As soon as I get home.'

'Don't tell me about your journey home, just about yourself.'

Peter understood the veiled message that anything he put in a letter would be censored.

'I understand,' he said, as he picked up his two bags and walked towards the waiting official.

'Here's your boarding pass,' the man said. 'We've endorsed your passport. Just leave your bag with me and you can walk straight through the exit over there.'

Ticket to Tallinn

The official led Peter through a narrow exit which was guarded by two armed soldiers. He spoke to one of the soldiers, who picked up Peter's suitcase and carried it towards the check-in counter for Tallinn.

'Do you wish to travel with your briefcase?'

'Yes, it's my one piece of hand luggage.'

Minutes later the soldier returned with a baggage label and Peter was led past the milling crowds and into the departure lounge.

'May I sit with you?'

Peter hadn't bargained for this. 'Yes, if you would like to.'

'Have you ever been to Tallinn before?'

'No, never.'

'It's very beautiful.'

'So I understand.'

'Of course, just now the people have caught the fever of our late comrades in the Eastern bloc. They agitate for independence, but we can never allow it.'

'Why's that?'

'Because they are an integral part of the USSR. They have been ruled by Russia since 1710.'

Peter looked up at him. The man's eyes were glinting behind his spectacles. He was a small, neat little man and Peter sensed that he was not only intelligent but that he also held a position of considerable authority. In what? he asked himself. The KGB?

'But I thought that on 24 February 1918 Estonia was proclaimed an independent country.'

'So you know a little of the history of Estonia.'

'Yes, I read about it before I came here.'

52

'Unfortunately your history book was not accurate. We never acknowledged that independence. Of course the Germans occupied the country from 1941-1944. That was brutal aggression.'

'Really?' exclaimed Peter, who had read a great deal about Estonia before his visit. 'I thought that your minister Molotov and Ribbentrop of Nazi Germany signed a pact in August 1939 which agreed the future status of Estonia as well as other European countries. I believe that there was also a secret protocol which concerned the three Baltic States.'

'Do you really believe that?' The official was staring intently and unblinkingly at Peter.

'I have read about it.'

'Don't believe everything you read, Mister Peter.' The hard cold eyes glinted even more intently as the man lent over towards him. 'A great deal of what you read is propaganda which is designed to stir up trouble and hatred of the USSR.'

'I see,' said Peter innocently. 'I never understood.

'I think that maybe you are in need of a little corrective education.'

'There's no time for that, I'm afraid.'

'I know, but I strongly advise you to keep your incorrect and inaccurate conclusions strictly to yourself when you are in Estonia. You will be very wise not to talk to anyone about your erroneous ideas.'

'I understand.'

'Good, I'm so glad. It would be unfortunate if you talked to anyone about them.' The man rose to leave. 'Goodbye, Mister Peter, and remember my advice.'

Chapter 4
Like any other Spy

For most of the flight Peter reflected on the conversation with the man in the airport lounge. He knew that he had said too much, and that he had betrayed the fact that he took more than a passing interest in the politics of the Baltic states. But the man's thinly veiled threats were ominous. He felt sure that the authorities knew more about his recent activities than he realised. He was worried, and was once again cursing himself for being naïve and foolish; he had got himself involved in political matters which were not his concern. At least I did not bring out a religious manuscript, he thought to himself. He felt his rolled up sleeve inside his jacket. The little roll of film was still safely inside it.

As the plane was shortly about to land he started to think about who would meet him and where he would be staying. He had been told that a Colonel Ivanovitch from COP would meet him, but he had no idea where he would be sleeping that night.

He soon discovered that Tallinn airport was even more chaotic and disorganised than the one in Moscow. The queue for immigration control was long, extremely slow-moving, and serviced by only two booths. It took forty minutes of dreary waiting before he reached one of them and when he did he was tired, frustrated and his head was throbbing from the effects of the last few hours. He handed over his blue *Laissez Passer*. The man

Like any other Spy

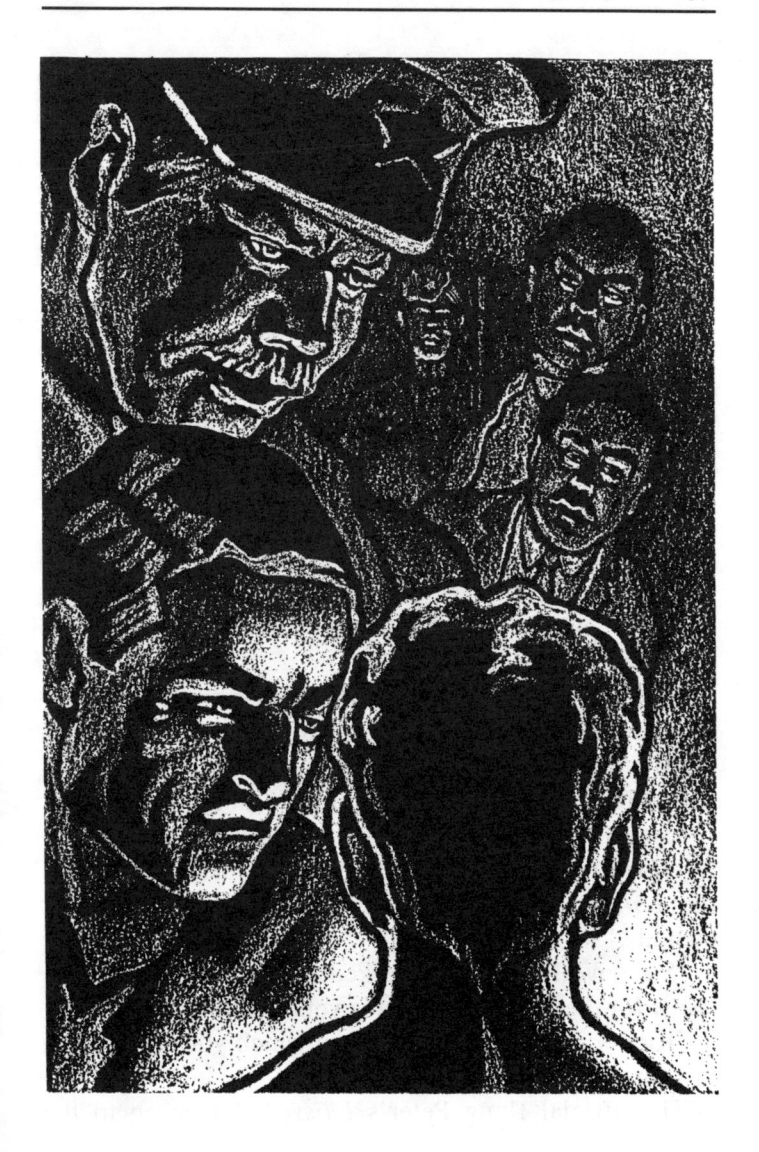

behind the counter took it and placed it under a shelf so that Peter could not see what he was looking at.

After some minutes of page-turning and intense concentration the uniformed official finally looked up at him, an unpleasant expression on his face.

'Where is your visa? What is your name?'

'I don't understand. You have it printed on the document in front of you.'

'Are you joking with me?'

'Of course not. Please, kindly stamp my *Laissez Passer* and allow me to go through.'

To Peter's surprise the man got up from his chair and without a word left the booth. Moments later he returned with two men, a senior official and an armed soldier.

'Come with us, please,' said the official. 'We need to question you.'

'Hey, just a minute,' said Peter heatedly. 'The passport gives me immunity.'

'It give you nothing of the sort. Please come.'

Peter had no alternative but to follow them into a room which was furnished with a table and two chairs. A large picture of Lenin hung crookedly on the wall.

'Sit down, please, and tell us your name.'

'Tell you my name! Can't you read what is printed on the *Laissez Passer*? It's written in English in block capitals.'

'Sit down!' the man barked at him. Peter obeyed. 'Now for the last time. What is your name?'

'Kindly read it in the document which you are holding in your right hand.'

The official flung Peter's *Laissez Passer* on to the

Like any other Spy

table. 'Very well,' he said, 'you read it to me.'

Peter picked up his *Laissez Passer* and opened it. It was blank. Completely blank. Not a single page had a scrap of detail. No name, no address, no history of previous travel. No stamps, no visa, nothing.

'I don't understand,' said Peter, utterly bewildered. 'Someone has changed the pages. I have been tricked.'

'I repeat. What is your name?'

'Peter Wade.'

'And why have you come to Tallinn? What business has brought you here without either a valid passport or a visa? I am sure that you know perfectly well that although Estonia is an integral part of the Soviet Union a visa is required for entry purposes.'

'Yes, I do. I'm telling you that I did have a valid passport. I wouldn't otherwise have been allowed to enter the Soviet Union. Someone in the USSR has tampered with my *Laisez Passer*, removed the pages and substituted them with blanks.'

'What is in your briefcase?'

'My private papers.'

'Show me, please.'

Peter unlocked his briefcase and the official went through his papers and belongings one by one. 'So you have come to visit COP on behalf of your organisation?'

'That is correct.'

'How long have you been in the USSR?'

Peter had little alternative but to answer the official's questions. At one point his suitcase was brought in and this too was unlocked and searched. Peter was anxious lest they make a body search and after an hour of intense

Ticket to Tallinn

questioning his worst fears were realised.

'And now we would like to search you.'

'I protest. I want to see an official from the British Embassy.'

'You can see one later. First you will be searched. Strip to your underpants please. We are totally within our rights to ask you to do this. If you want to telephone your embassy they will confirm it.'

Peter took off his jacket and trousers. They searched them thoroughly. Then he took off his shirt, which he dropped casually on the floor. The soldier picked it up and searched the pocket.

'What are these numbers on the back of this card?' the official enquired, handing Peter the card on which he had written down the London telephone number given to him by Roger. The soldier put down the shirt and looked over the official's shoulder to see the numbers for himself. 'What do they signify, Mr Wade?'

'They are the numbers of my credit card.'

'Where is your credit card, please?'

'I don't have it with me.'

'Why not?'

'Because it's of little use to me in the USSR.'

'It can buy a plane ticket if you're stranded.'

'I brought traveller's cheques.'

'Why?'

'To have money to spend, for God's sake. You can't question me in this way. I will make a formal protest to our government. Who do you think you are?'

'And just who do you think you are?' replied the official coldly. 'Attempting to enter a part of the USSR

Like any other Spy

without valid authority is a serious crime punishable by imprisonment. Get dressed. We'll keep this card.'

Peter realised that if he made too much fuss about the numbers they would become suspicious. He thought he could remember them, but at the moment that was a minor detail. What mattered was that the roll of film was still tucked inside his shirtsleeve. If they discovered that, he knew he could easily find himself inside a Soviet prison cell.

The official then said something which shed some light on his predicament.

'I understand that you are a student of Soviet history.'

'I beg your pardon?'

'I understand that you have taken an interest in the often repeated lie that a pact was signed between Mr Molotov of the USSR and Herr Ribbentrop of Nazi Germany before the Second World War, a pact which placed our beloved country under the perpetual rule of the USSR. Of course the reverse is true. For reasons of security the Estonian people embraced communism and placed themselves under the benevolent rule of the Soviet Union.'

So the man in Moscow had been in touch with them. What an idiot I am, Peter thought to himself. Can I never learn to keep my mouth shut?

'If you are referring to the conversation I had with an official at Moscow airport, forget it. That was a one off.'

'A one off? I don't understand the expression. It has not escaped our notice that you have taken an unhealthy and misguided interest in our historical affairs.'

'Like any other tourist or businessman.'

59

'Like any other spy.' The man spat out the word.

'Are you insinuating …?'

'I insinuate nothing. Get dressed. You will spend the night in the airport lock-up. Tomorrow you can contact your embassy official.'

Peter got dressed and was then led away to a smaller room which had a bed, a lavatory, and more ominously a peep-hole in the door. The room was brightly lit.

'Sleep well, Mr Wade.'

The door was banged shut and locked.

Peter woke the next morning with a bad taste in his mouth and an aching head. At eight o'clock a bad-tempered official brought him tea and stale toast, and told him that they had been in contact with the British embassy on his behalf. However, as the British had no consular representation in Tallinn, whoever was sent to interview him would have to travel from Moscow.

'When is he expected in Tallinn?' Peter asked.

'We have no idea,' the man replied.

At one o'clock he was given meat, potatoes, black bread and cold tea; at three o'clock, Mr de Melton, the First Secretary, arrived from the British Embassy in Moscow. He was a tall, neatly dressed man who meticulously copied down Peter's answers to his questions into a black leather notebook.

Peter told him the whole story, including the contact from the man called Roger, but carefully omitted to say anything about the roll of film. When he had finished, Mr de Melton spread out the fingers of each hand and inspected them very carefully one by one. Then he slowly raised his head and asked, 'Are you sure that you

Like any other Spy

have told me everything you know?'

'Quite sure.'

'If that's true, then I can't think why they went to the trouble of tampering with your *Laissez Passer*.'

'I think that it was done when I visited the monastery in Zagorsk. They had plenty of time to do it there and stupidly I never checked my *Laissez Passer* when they handed it back to me.'

'In that case they must have been worried about you long before you had your conversation with the official at Moscow airport.'

'That was stupid of me.'

'Have you taken a special interest in Estonian politics?'

'No. No more so than the average person who makes a visit to Estonia.'

'The question of Estonian independence is a very touchy subject at the moment.'

'I don't think that I'd be sitting in this room talking to you if it wasn't a touchy subject,' Peter said.

'Well, they haven't found out anything except for those numbers which you wrote down on your card. Do they really tally with your credit card, because that can easily be checked?'

'No,' Peter said, searching feverishly in his mind for a good excuse that might convince Mr de Melton. 'It's the telephone number of a girlfriend.'

Mr de Melton stared at him. 'Of course, they can check on that too. What's her name?'

'Rosemary Watson.'

'Why did you write the number down backwards?

Ticket to Tallinn

Isn't that a rather unusual thing to do?'

'Not when there is another girlfriend involved.'

Mr de Melton made a lengthy note in his pocketbook.

'Well, Mr Wade, if everything you've told me is true, then we should be able to get you out of here within the hour. Provided that Miss Rosemary Watson is able to verify your story.' He raised his eyebrows. 'Do you think that she'll be able to?'

'As long as she's at home,' Peter replied uneasily.

'It seems to me that they destroyed the pages in your *Laissez Passer* to give them an opportunity to check up thoroughly on what you are doing here. It provided them with an excuse to detain you. But if it was done at the monastery as you suspect, then they must have had you under observation ever since your arrival. Can you think of any reason why they would want to do that?'

'No.'

Mr de Melton lowered his voice. 'Your friend at COP, Victor Bogdanov, is minor KGB. We've known that for a long time. He is also unreliable and tries to keep in with everyone at the same time. I suspect that he's been detailed to check up on your activities.'

'But why should he? As I told you, we reached an agreement on a trading transaction.'

'That was an unwise thing to do, because it immediately places you in a vulnerable position. You were particularly ill-advised to sign a business document with an official. However, nothing is certain these days, and even the KGB are hedging their bets. It could be that Victor was not intending to frame you, but was trying to get a foot in the door of the market economy as a

Like any other Spy

safeguard against the future. Every other official seems to be trying to do that at the moment. If that is the case, then that particular piece of damning information will not be used against you.' He paused and turned away from Peter. 'The political situation is very fluid.'

'I have been told that.'

'It's true. Everyone is looking after their own interest as well as doing their official job. The more I think about it, the more convinced I am that it's Victor who got you into this mess.'

'But the agreement which he signed was in my briefcase. They must have read it.'

'I am sure they did. But you see, they are all into illegal deals in some form or other. They have obviously turned a blind eye to that agreement or you would have been confronted with it before now. That's what makes me so convinced that Victor is the man who framed you. But I must go. We have to do something about getting you out of here.'

And with those words, Mr de Melton left. Two hours later he returned with the official who had detained and questioned Peter.

'Mr Wade,' the Russian began, 'we are prepared to release you and have provided you with temporary documents. You may stay in Tallinn until tomorrow to finish your business here. We have arranged for you to fly out on tomorrow evening's flight to London via Stockholm. However, I must advise you that during your stay in Estonia you will be closely observed to see that you don't involve yourself in activities which are not conducive to the public good. I wish you a pleasant

Ticket to Tallinn

stay.'

Peter got up and shook his hand. He was handed temporary travel documents, a ticket, his suitcase and briefcase.

'Do you wish to change before you leave?' the official asked Peter.

'No, thank you. I will wait until I reach the hotel.'

'Good. Enjoy your stay in Estonia.'

'Thank you.'

'And by the way, neither the credit card company nor your girlfriend answered the telephone at the number which you gave us. Incidentally, do you read Arabic?'

Peter looked at him in amazement. 'No. Why?'

'It just struck us as strange that you should have taken the trouble to write down backwards a number which was obviously a phone number and not a credit card number. We will keep ringing until we get an answer.'

Peter was feeling uncomfortable after that conversation and he settled gratefully into the embassy car.

'I didn't like those last few questions.'

'Of course you didn't. I only hope that you've told me everything you know. Have you?'

Mr de Melton looked at him with piercing blue eyes. Peter met the stare.

'Everything,' he said.

They drove into the old town. 'They have put you into the Rataskaevu Hotel. It's a quaint old place, and not bad value for money. I think that your COP contact will be waiting for you. Watch him. He's ex-military and possibly minor KGB. I expect that he won't let you out of his sight and that he has strict orders to monitor your

64

Like any other Spy

every move. He won't have the authority to fix the dates of your visitor's trip to Estonia. That can only come from Moscow, and from your recent experience there, you are not likely to get an authorisation for their visit for some time to come.'

'Which will have made my visit a waste of time.'

Mr de Melton gave him another cold stare. 'I'm sorry about that.'

Peter noted the hint of disbelief in the reply but said nothing. Mr de Melton had been an invaluable help and it would be unwise to upset him. They stopped outside the hotel and Peter grasped Mr de Melton firmly by the hand. 'I can't thank you enough.'

'Just doing my job. But take care. If you get into trouble again it won't be so easy to get you out of it.'

'Don't worry. I'll try to look after myself.' Peter picked up his luggage and walked towards the hotel. As soon as he was inside, a small athletic figure with a crooked grin and shabby clothes walked up to him.

'Mister Peter? I'm Colonel Ivanovitch, but you can call me Ivan.'

Peter looked hard at Ivan. He seemed to be about fifty and had the bearing of an old soldier and of someone who was loyal to the old communist order.

'Good to meet you, Ivan. I'm sorry I'm late but I was unavoidably delayed.'

'Yes, I know, they informed me at the airport. I was waiting for you there. Is everything okay now?'

'Just fine,' Peter replied non-committally.

'I've fixed your programme for tomorrow, starting at nine o'clock. We can have dinner together tonight at the hotel. I live in Pirita which is some distance away, so I have booked myself into this hotel. In fact, I have the room next to yours.'

Which leaves absolutely nothing to chance, thought Peter. I'm going to be lucky if I can visit the Sweet Tooth Café on my own.

Ivan led Peter to his room, which was clean, tidy and much less noisy than his room in Moscow. 'I'm just next door if you need me,' Ivan said with a grin. 'I'll see you at nine. Knock on my door when you are ready.'

Peter was already beginning to feel like a prisoner with his jailer sleeping next door. As he returned to his room he began to make a thorough search. He started in the bathroom, then he moved into the bedroom. He looked carefully under the bed and around the bedstead. Then he went over to the window. At last he found what he was looking for. Fitted snugly behind the curtain rail was a concealed microphone with a wire running into the wall of the next-door room – where Ivan no doubt lay listening to his every move. He took out a pocket-knife and cut the wire.

'Sorry, Ivan,' he said. 'But you should thank me. You're now going to have an undisturbed night's sleep.'

At precisely nine o'clock Peter left his room. As he passed Ivan's door it opened and out came the Colonel, who followed him down the stairs and into the dining room. They settled down at a table for two.

'So what would you like to do while you are in Tallinn?' Ivan asked after they had given the waiter their order.

Peter looked at him intently. 'As you know,' he began,

Like any other Spy

'I have come to finalise the visit of our team of environmental experts.'

'Ah yes, the visit,' said Colonel Ivan, turning away from Peter's gaze. 'I think it might be difficult for us to finalise that at the moment.'

'That hardly surprises me,' said Peter. 'If the COP couldn't make a decision in Moscow, it's hardly likely that you would be allowed to make one here.'

'Are you implying that we have to refer decisions of this nature to Moscow?'

'Of course. Isn't Estonia totally subservient to Moscow?'

The Colonel hesitated before replying, then he said very slowly, 'That is the current situation. However, we are working to change it.'

'Are you?'

'I think, Mister Peter, that we should not pursue the conversation further,' said the Colonel uneasily. 'Naturally I cannot discuss matters of delicate political importance with you. The central government in Moscow will do what is best for Estonia.'

You little creep, Peter thought, I know who gives you your orders and they don't come out of Tallinn.

The waiter brought their meal, a simple stew, and they ate it in silence. His recent experience with customs and immigration had not left Peter in a mood for polite conversation. After plums and watered-down milk the Colonel said, 'I suggest that we arrange to meet at the COP office at nine o'clock tomorrow. I will collect you at eight-thirty.'

Peter decided to be bold. 'I don't see the point.'

Ticket to Tallinn

'I don't understand.'

'I said, I don't see the point. You've already said that the one thing on which I need a decision, the timing of the visit, cannot be discussed because there's no one in Tallinn with the authority to authorise it. I might as well go sight-seeing.'

'But they are expecting you at the office. I have arranged a programme.'

'Too bad, there's nothing to discuss.'

Peter knew that he was not only being rude, but also that by behaving in this way he was possibly ensuring that the visit would never take place at all. But he had to ensure that he could visit the Sweet Tooth Café, and as he had to fly out the next evening he didn't want to be delayed in a dreary office making empty small talk.

Colonel Ivan was looking at him through narrowed eyes. He had been ordered not to let Mister Peter out of his sight and that was an easy task when they were seated round a table in an office. Wandering with him around the sights of Tallinn was another matter.

'But …'

'No "buts", Ivan. Tell your colleagues that either we hold a meeting which decides on a definite date for the visit, or I will see the sights of Tallinn.'

Colonel Ivan capitulated. 'All right. What time would you like to leave the hotel?'

'Nine-thirty. But I'm quite capable of visiting the old city on my own.'

'That is not possible. I have to look after you. We don't want you to become involved in any difficult situations.'

Peter smiled. 'That's kind of you,' he said

Like any other Spy

sarcastically. 'I look forward to your company.'

And on that note of mutual suspicion and hostility they parted and went to their rooms, the Colonel making quite certain that Peter was locked up in his room before retiring to his own.

After breakfasting, Peter left his room at nine-thirty. As he passed the Colonel's door it opened.

'Good morning, did you sleep well?'

'Very well, thanks, Ivan. I hope you didn't lie awake all night waiting for me to leave my room.'

'I managed to get some sleep, thank you.'

'It must be a difficult job.'

'I don't understand.'

'Keeping watch on me twenty-four hours a day.'

'Do you know what you would like to see in Tallinn?'

'Yes, I would like to see St Olai's church, which my guidebook says was built in the thirteenth century and was once considered to have the tallest tower in the world. Then I would like to visit the Great Guild Hall and some of the medieval houses in Pikk Street. Then I thought that I could treat you to lunch at the Maiasmokk café which I believe is called 'Sweet Tooth' in English.'

'You seem to have studied your guidebook well.'

'Are you still sure that you want to come with me?'

Ivan smiled. 'Don't play games, Mister Peter.'

They set off for the church, its tower now much reduced in height by fire and lightning, but nonetheless an impressive and prominent landmark in Tallinn. The guide explained that when the master builder had at last finished building the tower he gazed down at the people below, lost his footing and crashed to the ground. When the unfortunate man hit the road beneath the tower, a toad and a snake came out of his mouth.

After leaving St Olai's church they walked around the remains of the city wall, visited three guild houses and the Great Guild Hall, now a museum depicting life in Tallinn through the ages. Finally, at twelve-thirty, they reached the Maiasmokk café in Pikk Street.

'This was a famous café before the Second World War,' Ivan explained. 'Under the new liberalisation, the authorities have recently allowed it to re-open as a café.'

'The Estonian people must be very grateful to the Soviet Union,' said Peter sarcastically.

Ivan, who did not understand the nature of Peter's sarcasm, agreed.

Peter followed him in to the café. It was small and freshly whitewashed and had a high vaulted ceiling. There were about twelve tables, of which half were occupied. A waiter approached them as they entered, and as he drew close Peter immediately recognised him. It was Vladimir.

'We would like a table for two,' said Ivan in Russian. Since Peter's arrival he had not attempted to speak to anyone in Estonian.

Vladimir led them to a table which was standing on its own, away from the other diners. Not a flicker of recognition crossed his face and Peter, after the initial shock of seeing him, tried to avoid his eyes.

'That will do fine,' said Ivan.

When they were seated Peter said, 'This meal is on me, Ivan. Please order what you want.' Moments later

Ticket to Tallinn

Vladimir came over to them with a menu.

'I'm sorry, comrades, but today we unfortunately only have soup to start with. However, I can highly recommend it. It contains fresh vegetables.'

'But I can see someone eating shrimps over there,' queried Ivan.

'Yes, but sadly they are now all finished.'

Ivan grumbled about this but decided to take the soup followed by salted herring. Peter ordered the same.

'Would you like to see the wine list? We have a very good Estonian white wine.'

'I don't think that I will,' Ivan began.

'Of course you will,' Peter cut in. 'I insist.'

The soup arrived after a short interval, brought to the table by a pretty girl in Estonian national dress. She placed the steaming hot bowl on the table and began to ladle it into two plates. Setting one plate in front of Peter she picked up the other and moved to put it in front of Ivan. As she did so she appeared to slip and the hot bowl of soup flew out of her hands and tipped upside down into Ivan's lap. At this point it became difficult to make out who screamed the loudest – the waitress out of fear or Ivan out of pain. He leapt to his feet and with a great yell began to tear at his shirt and trousers.

The café manager rushed forward uttering apologies to Ivan and dire threats at the unfortunate girl, who was now reduced to floods of tears. Taking Ivan by the arm, the manager led him away to change his shirt and trousers. No sooner had he disappeared through a door at the back of the café than Vladimir was at Peter's side.

'Do you still have the film?' he whispered anxiously.

Like any other Spy

'Yes.'

'Thank God.' He slipped a small package into Peter's hand. 'This is another film, just as important as the other one. Guard it with your life. There is also a new telephone number for you to ring in London.' He deliberately raised his voice. 'I do apologise for the terrible inconvenience we have caused.'

'Thank you,' said Peter equally loudly. 'It was an accident, of course, but I do hope that my friend has not been badly burnt.' As he was talking Peter slipped the packet into his pocket. 'Where is the lavatory, please?'

'Over there, comrade, follow me.' He lowered his voice. 'Take care, it's bugged.'

Vladimir led Peter over to the lavatory, and once inside Peter took off his coat and opened the package. There was a film inside and a new telephone number which he memorised. He tucked the film into his right-hand shirt sleeve, and flushed the wrapping paper and the paper with the number on it down the lavatory. Then he hurried back to his table. Five minutes later Ivan appeared, red in the face and wearing borrowed clothes. He was furious.

'Are you all right?'

'Yes, I'm all right and not badly scalded. But I'm going to report this incident to the authorities,' he said loudly enough for all the diners to hear. 'I will see that this café is closed. It is a scandal. It is a great scandal.' He eyed Peter closely. 'And what about you?'

'What do you mean?'

'What about you? What have you been doing?'

'Waiting for you so that we could resume our lunch.'

73

Ticket to Tallinn

They ate in silence. Ivan was so angry that he could hardly bring himself to speak to Peter. But whether that was on account of the soup or the fact that Peter had managed to escape his attention for a few minutes Peter could not make out.

They walked slowly back to the hotel. 'I enjoyed that,' Peter said. 'I hope that next time I come we'll be able to finalise the dates of the visit. I'm sorry that I didn't meet your colleagues but I didn't see the point.'

'There won't be a next time for you,' said the Colonel coldly. 'You will not be given a visa.'

Peter said nothing. There was no point in antagonising the man further.

'I will watch you pack,' Ivan continued. 'You will allow me into your room.'

Peter shrugged his shoulders. 'All right,' he said, 'if you enjoy that sort of thing, come in by all means.'

When they reached Peter's room Ivan followed him inside and sat gloomily on the bed, watching his every move.

'You found the bug.'

'Yes, I'm sorry I spoilt your fun, but I'm sure that it was better for you to have had a good night's sleep.'

Ivan went over to the window and inspected the severed wire. 'You are playing a dangerous game,' he said as he studied the broken fitting.

'I'm not playing games, Ivan. I just want to get home.'

'Are you taking a shower?'

'Of course, and you can search my bag while I am taking it, if that's what you want to do.'

Like any other Spy

Peter walked over to the bathroom, undressed and showered. He then replaced his original clothing and reappeared to find Ivan bent over his suitcase.

'Found anything of interest?'

'No, not yet.'

'Don't worry, there's nothing to find. Do you enjoy your work, Ivan? I suppose as a dedicated Russian you must do.'

'I'm not a Russian,' said Ivan. 'I'm Estonian. We do not all desire the freedom from Russian rule that you seem to think we do.'

'I suppose if you are paid enough you will do anything,' said Peter, adjusting his tie in the mirror. 'Come, let's go, Ivan. The taxi I ordered should be here by now, and I know that you won't be happy until you see me safely on board the plane.'

At the airport the authorities seemed to be even more anxious than Ivan to get rid of Peter. He was ushered through customs and emigration at breakneck speed. Once again his suitcase and briefcase were thoroughly searched. Once again his rolled up shirt sleeves protected the rolls of film.

'Disappointed?' he asked Ivan as they shook hands for the last time. 'Disappointed that you can't pin anything on me?'

'Every Estonian wishes you good luck,' Ivan replied, to Peter's utter amazement.

'Ivan. I thought that ...'

But Ivan was already pushing his way through the crowd and was well out of earshot. Peter stared after him in amazement, then turned to board the plane.

Ticket to Tallinn

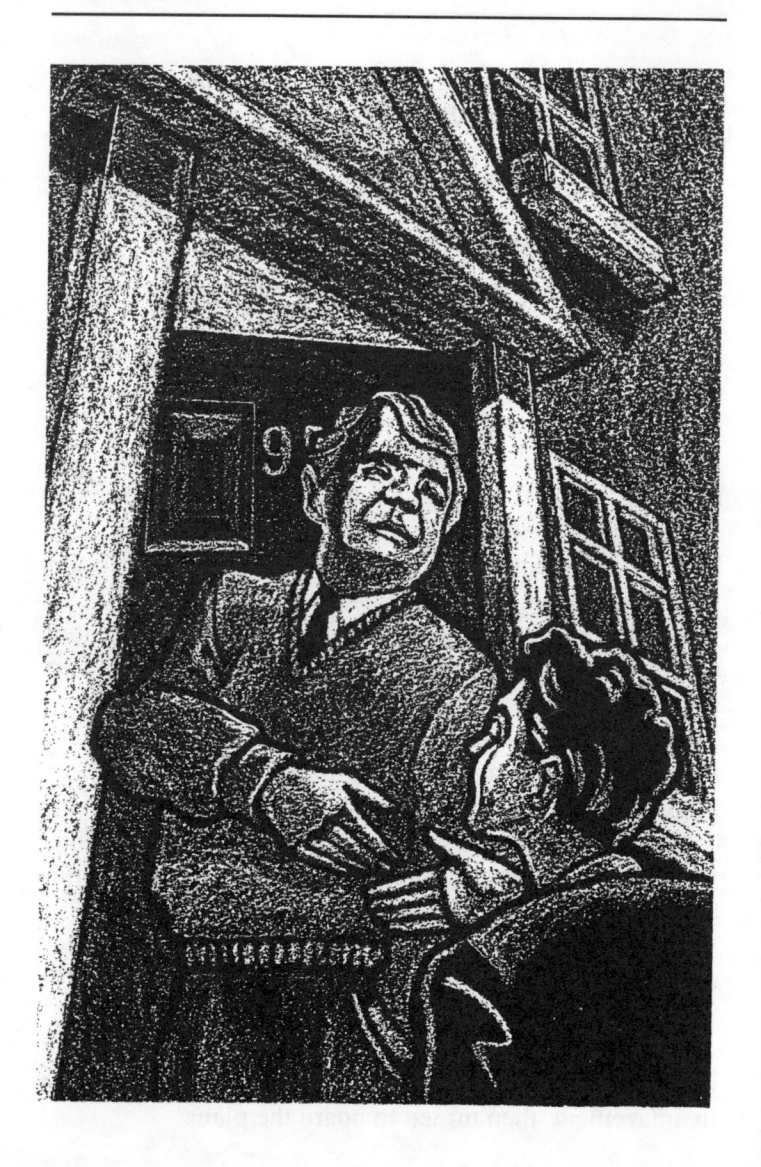

Chapter 5

Congratulations

Ninety-five Lennox Gardens was a red brick, four-storeyed house in an expensive part of London. At precisely twelve o'clock the following morning, Richard Dawes, the owner of the property, was to be found at his front door holding out a hand of welcome to Peter. He was a grey-haired, middle-aged man with a bronzed and somewhat battered face, and he was dressed in denim trousers and a red pullover. He gave Peter a smile and invited him into a tastefully furnished sitting room.

Before Peter had time to say anything he asked: 'Have you brought the film?'

'Yes.'

'Congratulations. You don't know it but you have earned the undying gratitude of millions of Estonians, and possibly a few million more Lithuanians and Latvians as well. Believe me when I tell you that what you have done is of historic significance.'

Peter sank into a leather armchair and looked up at the stranger who had invited him round as soon as he had rung the telephone number given to him by Vladimir.

'Perhaps you can kindly explain ...'

'Of course. It was impossible to explain to you before but now that you have completed your impossible mission I can tell all.'

'Before you begin, can I ask you one question? Has there ever been any intention of our sending a mission of experts to check on Chernobyl, or was that a non-starter from the beginning?'

'Totally. The Russians may be liberalising in some respects, but they are much too sensitive about Chernobyl and their secrets in Estonia to allow a group of foreign experts to go prying about. Although your agency didn't know it, there was never a hope that the visit would take place. But we did want someone to travel to Moscow and Tallinn – someone who was on a legitimate non-governmental mission. So we put it about that a mission would be allowed to take place and would be successful. You were an ideal candidate.'

'Why?'

'Because you have had no previous connection with either the USSR or Estonia, and you are working for a respectable organisation. You see, Galina, Natasha and Vladimir all have strong loyalties to the cause of Estonian independence. Their boss, Victor, is minor KGB, and, as I suspect you have guessed, is ready to hedge his bets by dabbling in the market economy. Galina deliberately encouraged him to sign a commercial deal with you so that he could, if necessary, be compromised by sending the evidence to his boss in the KGB. Petty officials turn a blind eye when they see evidence of the illegal market economy at work, but a senior KGB man would take a different view. However, Victor became suspicious that both Galina and her daughter were getting you to do something for them. So

Congratulations

he decided both to find out what they were up to and to fix you, by deliberately ensuring that your blank *Laissez Passer* would result in a thorough customs search. The search took place, but nothing was found except a telephone number, which, fortunately for all of us, was out of order when they tried to reach it from Tallinn. Meanwhile, Vladimir had tested your willingness to help the cause by talking to you about the religious manuscript at the circus. When he realised that you were not totally averse to taking material out of the country, he knew that they had a good chance of persuading you to bring out the film. As he has an Estonian passport, he was able to slip back to Tallinn and obtain a temporary job in the Maisamokk café and give you the other film to bring out of Estonia.'

'And the monk?'

'He is an Estonian too – the cleaner is his mother.'

'I think I understand everything except the most important question of all. What is on this film?'

Peter handed the two rolls of film to Mr Dawes.

'That, Peter, is something the world, or at least an interested part of it, has been waiting for, for a very long time. You see, when the pact between Nazi Germany and the Soviet Union was signed in 1941 there was in addition a top secret protocol. Its existence was known, but no one in the West had seen the document. Effectively, it agreed to the division of Eastern Europe between the Russians and the Germans; but in particular it shows that Germany accepted that the three Baltic Republics should be placed under the sphere of influence of the Soviet Union. Two months ago, quite by accident, an Estonian official working in the Soviet archives came across the secret protocol. He was able to photograph the complete document and return it to the archives without being detected. As soon as this was accomplished it became imperative to get the film out of the Soviet Union as quickly as possible. Galina is a trusted Estonian agent. Her daughter has a boyfriend who doubled as Roger. The film was passed to Galina and I suspect that you know the rest.'

'But what about the other film that was given to me by Vladimir in Tallinn? What does that contain?'

'That film contains a copy of another document which was also thought to have been lost and which was discovered in the archives in Tallinn. A copy of the treaty which the USSR signed with the three Baltic States in 1920, and which renounced "for all times" any Soviet claim to sovereignty over the Baltic States.'

'So on the one hand, there is the treaty formalising their independence for all time, and on the other hand, a later secret treaty with Germany which placed the three Baltic Republics under Soviet control.'

'Exactly, and you can now see how important these two documents are to the three Republics, when they are currently fighting for world recognition of their just claim to independence from Soviet authority.'

'I don't see how the world can deny them that status once these two documents are published.'

'It will come in time, and when it does, you can take comfort from the fact that you played an important part in their fight for freedom. But meanwhile, would you like a stiff drink? You deserve it.'